A Cat's
Night Before
Christmas

Sue Carabine

Illustrations by
Shauna Mooney Kawasaki

GIBBS·SMITH
PUBLISHER

SALT LAKE CITY

04 03 02 01   10 9 8 7

Copyright © 1996 Gibbs Smith, Publisher

Printed in Hong Kong

Published by
Gibbs Smith, Publisher
P.O. Box 667
Layton, Utah 84041

ISBN 0-87905-761-0
ISBN 1-58685-124-1/GIFT

'Twas the night
before Christmas;
kids were
tucked up in bed.

They couldn't
help thinking of
what Mama had said.

What was it again?
Oh, "The fog's
thick as stew.

"I hope that St. Nicholas
can make his way
through."

Not only the children
could hear
Mama's words,

But Mittens,
curled up in the chair,
also heard.

Her sharp ears
perked up,
and she opened one eye.

"No Santa—no catnip,"
she thought
with a sigh.

"Out here in the East,
Santa Claus starts
his trip,"

Mittens said to herself
while licking
her lips.

"Why isn't he here?
His milk's getting warm.

If he doesn't come soon
I will sound the alarm."

When the
cuckoo clock chirped
that the time
was midnight,

Mittens slid through
her pet door,
knowing things were
not right.

She mewed for her pal
who lived in the alley;

Old Brutus and she
must come up
with a rally.

They huddled together
to make a
decision,

Then scampered away
to accomplish
their mission.

Very soon
the word spread
through cities
and towns,

From the east coast
of Maine
to the Wyoming Downs.

The secret was
whisssssspered
from one cat to another,

From females to toms,
and from kittens
to mothers.

To their watch posts
they went—
leaving comfort
at home—

From Persians
in Pittsburgh
to calicoes
in Nome.

On fence posts and
tree limbs,
on porches and roofs,

The Siamese and Persians
and Manx
made their moves.

They crouched there
all soundless
and gazed up at the sky,

In hopes they'd
soon hear
Santa's sleigh bells
on high.

In the meantime,
St. Nicholas
was getting
frustrated,

From dealing
with problems
This fog had created.

The sleigh
had been circling
for two hours or more,

Nick attempting to see
a tall chimney or door.

When, suddenly, he saw
an incredible sight:

His fog beams reflected
some almond-shaped
lights.

The cats' eyes,
like a runway,
were easy to follow,

So Santa and reindeer
took off like
Apollo.

As he called on
each home,
A cat lay in wait

To guide him along
so he wouldn't
be late.

From one to another
they purred
and meowed,

Till just before dawn
Santa finished somehow!

Then two little children,
with faces aglow,

Ran out to see where
their stockings
were stowed.

Passing Mittens,
they said,
"My, how lazy you are;

"You've not moved
from this spot,
or at least not too far."

But Santa
knew better,
as he soared
to the skies,

Watching millions
of homes
with cats snoozing
inside.

"They've truly
helped out.
Without them,
I believe,

We would never
have made it
on this
Christmas Eve.

"So, rest easy,
dear felines,
and thanks
for your trouble.

"Merry Christmas to all,
may your nine lives
be doubled!"